# NOBODY OWNS THE MOON

*For Number Three*
*(Airlie)*

Published in 2019 by Berbay Publishing Pty Ltd

PO Box 133
Kew East
Victoria 3102 Australia

Text and illustrations © Tohby Riddle

First published by Penguin Australia in 2008

The moral right of the author and illustrator has been asserted.

Printed by Everbest Printing in China.

National Library of Australia

Cataloguing-in publication data:
Riddle, Tohby

9780994384195

# NOBODY OWNS THE MOON

## Tohby Riddle

BERBAY
PUBLISHING

The fox is one of the only wild creatures in the world that can successfully make a life for itself in cities.

This is because
it is quick-witted...

and able to eat
a variety of foods.

Other creatures can live in cities, but often with limited success — especially when compared with the fox.

One fox who lives successfully in the city is
Clive Prendergast. Clive Prendergast is the name
he gave himself to fit better into his city world;
his real name can only be pronounced by foxes.

Clive lives in a small one-room apartment in a busy part of town.

By day, Clive works in a factory.
He doesn't know what is made there; he just puts
the same two parts together – over and over.

By night, Clive gets up to more foxy things.

He likes to slink about his streets and alleyways,
sniffing out odds and ends among the street stalls
and interesting goings-on.

One time he saw a dancing bear.

Clive keeps pretty much to himself. But he does have a friend or two. He probably sees his friend Humphrey the most. Humphrey's a donkey. He's one of those creatures that live in cities with less success than foxes.

Humphrey doesn't always
have a fixed address.

He's had the odd job but
he hasn't kept it for long.

His most recent job was as a piano removalist.

Clive often seeks out Humphrey on his days or nights off.
He likes Humphrey.

One day, Clive went looking for his friend. He found
him beneath a statue of a great conqueror.

Clive noticed that Humphrey looked a little worse
for wear. Like he hadn't eaten fresh food for some
time, or had a good sleep.

It was then that Clive noticed a
little blue envelope. It was among
Humphrey's things that he kept
in an old tote bag.

'Where'd you get that, Humphrey?' Clive asked,
pointing at the special-looking envelope.
'I found it in the gutter – the paper looked nice.'

Clive whisked it out of the bag
and looked more closely.
'You like it too?' asked Humphrey.
'I was going to eat it. But if you're
hungry, Clive, it's yours.'

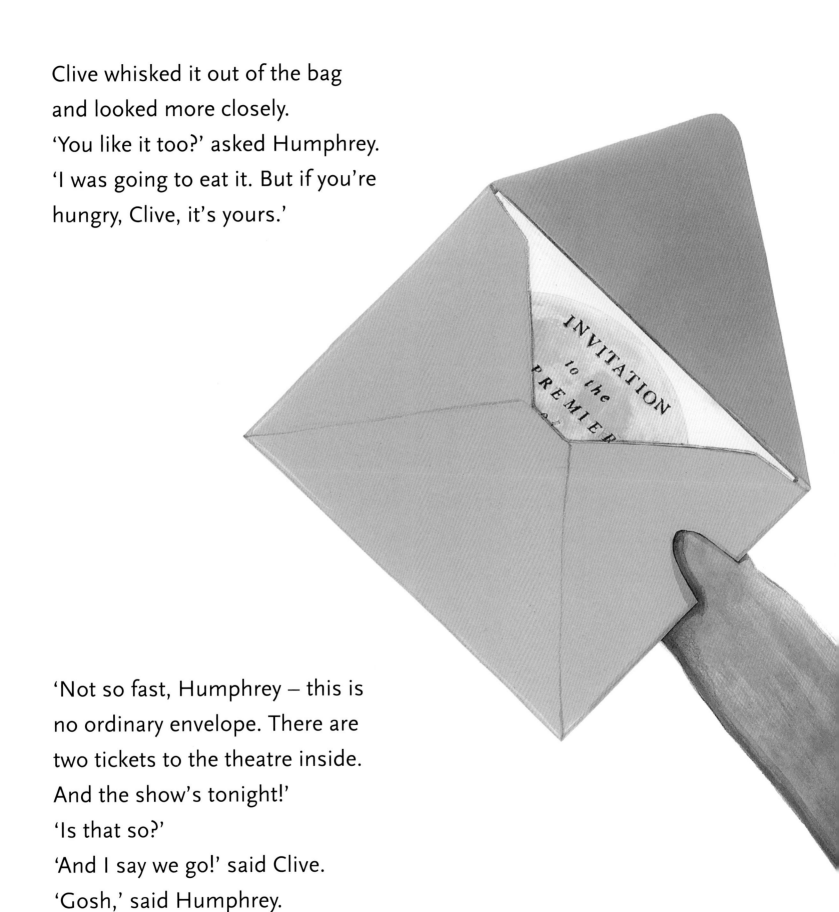

INVITATION
to the
PREMIER

'Not so fast, Humphrey – this is
no ordinary envelope. There are
two tickets to the theatre inside.
And the show's tonight!'
'Is that so?'
'And I say we go!' said Clive.
'Gosh,' said Humphrey.

That night Humphrey and Clive attended the premiere
of *Nobody Owns the Moon* – the latest play by the city's
most celebrated playwright.

They enjoyed the delicious hors d'oeuvres and the
marvellous punch that was served in the theatre's
glittering foyer beforehand.

Then they were ushered to luxurious dress circle seats where they could see absolutely everything.

Soon they were swept along by the sheer brilliance of *Nobody Owns the Moon*. In all the right places, they laughed and sighed, and as it neared its bittersweet ending, Humphrey wept.

Afterwards, they found that their tickets entitled them to a hot beverage of their choice and a large slice of cake in the theatre's elegant restaurant.

Humphrey wept again.

And that night, as Clive and Humphrey sauntered away —
off into the glimmering melee of lights and sounds that
was their city at night — they said to each other...

'This is our town!'

And when they got to the corner where they'd go their separate ways, Humphrey gave Clive a big hug goodnight.

*The End*